D1381978

THIS BOOK IS DEDICATED TO LUCA AND WILF

First published in Great Britain in 2013 by Simon and Schuster UK Ltd,
a CBS company.
Simon & Schuster UK Ltd
1st Floor, 222 Gray's Inn Road, London WC1X 8HB

www.simonandschuster.co.uk

Text copyright © Jack Carson 2013
With special thanks to Matt Whyman and Michelle Misra
Cover illustration copyright © Lorenzo Etherington 2013
Interior illustration copyright © Damien Jones 2013

The right of Jack Carson, Lorenzo Etherington and Damien Jones to be identified
as the author and illustrators of this work respectively has been asserted by them
in accordance with sections 77 and 78 of the Copyright,
Designs and Patents Act, 1988.

A CIP catalogue record for this book is available from the British Library.

PB ISBN: 978-0-85707-563-5
eBook ISBN: 978-0-85707-564-2

1 3 5 7 9 10 8 6 4 2

Printed and bound by CPI Group (UK) Ltd,
Croydon CR0 4YY

BATTLE CHAMPIONS

SWAMPLAND SLAM

JACK CARSON

SIMON AND SCHUSTER

THE CHAMPIONSHIP TRAIL

Prairie Territory

The Canyon

Mines

Rust Town

Badlands

Mines

OCEAN TERMINAL

Prologue

Sometime in the future, a war destroys the world as we know it. As people struggle to rebuild their lives, a new sport emerges from the ruins. In the Battle Championship, giant robots known as 'mechs' square up to one another and fight like gladiators. They're controlled from the inside by talented pilots, in a fight that tests man and machine to the limit.

All kids grow up dreaming of piloting a mech, and Titch Darwin is no exception. But for Titch it's personal. He's the son of one of the greatest Battle Champions – a man who went missing on the Championship trail – and the only way for Titch to find out what happened is to follow in his father's footsteps

1

Arrival

Titch and Martha looked up and around in awe. They had just followed a path through a tangle of creepers and trees to the edge of a very large swamp.

'Wow!' said Titch, a grin stretching across his freckled face. 'It's so peaceful.'

'Wait until the fighting starts here tomorrow!' said Martha. 'It won't be so quiet then!'

They had settled their things into a guesthouse on the edge of town before coming out to take a look at their next battleground. Rotting branches poked out of the murky brown water. Dragonflies flitted over the surface and frogs could be heard croaking all around. For a moment, the two friends watched the sun sink behind the trees. Then something stirred in the water just in front of them. It was only a ripple, but enough to draw their attention.

'What was that?' Titch ran a hand through his sandy hair.

'A fish?' suggested Martha.

And that's when the alligator exploded through the surface of the water.

'Whoa!' they cried, jumping back.

'We need to get out of here,' yelled Titch. 'Come on! Let's go!'

Titch was small for his age, but quick on his feet. Even so, as they spun around, he wasn't quite quick enough. A second alligator had crept along the path towards them. There was no place to go. The two friends were boxed in!

'Er, what do we do now?' asked Martha, starting to panic. 'This place is totally dangerous! I don't want to end up as a snack for that beast!'

Titch spun around, searching for a way out. Then he glanced back over his shoulder. The alligator in the swamp was gliding towards them.

'Nothing like a little danger to keep us on our toes!' he grinned.

'A little danger is fine,' muttered Martha. 'But this is way too much for my liking!'

Titch reached inside his jacket and pulled out a walkie-talkie.

'Hey, Finn, are you there?' Titch spoke quickly but calmly to the final member of their team. 'We're down at the water's edge and could do with a little help right now...' He stopped and waited for a response, but there was only a crackle of static. Slowly, his grin began to fade. 'Finn? Hello?'

'It's a bad time for my brother to be busy,' said Martha, switching her attention from one alligator to the other. 'You know what? It's time we ran!'

The pair looked around in search of a way out. To their dismay, they were hemmed in on both sides by steep banks choked with vegetation.

By now, the two alligators were side by side at the water's edge. Both prowled steadily towards them. Titch stopped and listened. He could just make out a noise of some sort over by the treeline. Then he saw a sudden swaying and snapping of branches, as if something very, very big was making its way towards them. Birds scattered into the air as the disturbance continued to grow. And then, before their eyes, a giant robot pushed out into the open. Even the alligators wheeled around!

The machine was as high as the tallest trees, with a head slung low on wide shoulders and a musclebound torso made of moulded metal panels. It moved on legs that were sprung at the knees and had been fitted with wide footplates to stop it from sinking into the boggy land. The alligators looked startled as the giant drew to a halt. Towering over the clearing, it stared down at them with burning red lamps for eyes.

'Better late than never,' said Martha, with a sigh of relief.

A boy could be seen behind a glass panel in the giant machine's chest. Strapped inside a cockpit, he was surrounded by panels of blinking lights, dials and switches, and seemed to be controlling the machine's movements.

'Finn!' Titch cried out. 'Wow, are we glad to see you!'

Finn and Martha were twins. Together with Titch, they had come to the swamp to fight it out in the next stage of a very special sport – the Battle Championship. This fighting machine – or mech – went by the name of LoneStar. When it was fitted with weapons, it was purpose-built to take on a whole range of competing mechs in knockdown fights. Just then, Titch prayed this particular mech could save their skin! When his walkie-talkie crackled into life, he swiftly pressed it to his ear.

'I suppose you guys would like a lift,' said Finn from the cockpit.

'Yes, we want a lift!' cried Martha, snatching the walkie-talkie from Titch. 'Why didn't you say anything when Titch tried to reach you just now? We thought you hadn't heard?'

'I had to reboot the system to get the communication link working,' said Finn. 'You're lucky I knew how to do it. As the test pilot, that's not my job. You're the mechanic, Martha. You really need to fix that before the first battle round!'

'Well, let's worry about that later,' said Martha as LoneStar dropped to its knees and reached a giant hand out towards them.

Titch and Martha wasted no time in scrambling into the giant's cupped palms. The alligators snapped at the machine, but there was nothing they could do. They slunk back into the swamp as quickly as they had appeared. Titch felt a jolt as LoneStar rose back onto its feet.

'Thanks for the ride!' He grinned at his

friend inside the cockpit.

'Hey, we're a team,' said Finn. 'I couldn't let our pilot come to any harm, could I? Not when we've come to this battleground to win!'

● ● ●

2

Good News and Bad News

The guesthouse was located in Crawfish Creek, a sleepy little fishing outpost, hemmed in by swampland. A one-horse track led in and out of the main street, where traders, trappers and loggers often came for supplies or to escape from the heat in the saloon bar. Not much happened here, except for one weekend each year – the Battle Championship weekend!

When the Championship came to town, every guesthouse was filled with the competitors and their crews. Across the main street, the park was fenced in and transformed into the Armoury – the place where each crew worked on fitting their mech with weapons to make sure they were battle-ready. As for the spectators – they camped out wherever they could before gathering in the grandstands around the swamp for the first of three knockout rounds.

'That was a close call,' said Titch, back at the guesthouse after their encounter with the alligators. He was sitting out on the porch with Martha and Finn. All of them were drinking from mugs of steaming hot chocolate, watching the moon rise over the trees. 'Still, at least we know that the footplates are perfect for this terrain,' he chuckled. 'I reckon this weekend could see a lot of mechs getting bogged down.'

'Well, let's hope your winning streak doesn't run out,' said Martha. 'I can't believe you're top of the leaderboard!'

'And we've only fought in one weekend of the Championship!' said Titch. 'Maybe I

18

just got lucky.'

'Luck, skill – who knows,' said Finn. 'Whatever the case, any competitor we're up against will want to take you down. When I put LoneStar away for the night in the Armoury, I overheard some pilots saying that a pipsqueak like you needed teaching a lesson.'

'Charming,' said Titch, shrugging his shoulders. 'I may be on the young side, but once I'm strapped inside LoneStar I feel like I can take on even the toughest competitors.'

'It's going to be tough,' Martha agreed. 'No doubt about it.'

Just then, their conversation was interrupted by the arrival of three men in green overalls whom Titch recognised from the previous weekend. 'It's the AntiGrav crew,' he reminded Titch and Martha as he stood up to greet the other competitors. 'How are you guys doing?'

'Not so good,' the first man said as

they trudged up the steps to the guest house. The crew were Battle Championship veterans. They had steered AntiGrav through many seasons and were favourites to win this weekend. Even so, the trio looked gloomy and downcast.

'Something wrong?' asked Martha.

'We were ambushed on the journey here,' said the pilot. 'We couldn't fight

back as our mech was in safety mode for the journey. They stole our machine at gunpoint. Took our horses, too. We've had to walk all this way.'

'But that's terrible!' cried Martha. Everyone knew the dangers when it came to travelling with mechs. They were highly-prized machines, after all, and the Championship trail often took them

across badlands.

'So where did this happen?' asked Finn.

'At Dismal Gorge,' said one of the men. Titch glanced at Finn. They had been warned to be on the lookout when passing through that region. With so many hiding places in the rocks, it was known to be a hangout for desperadoes. Earlier that day, Finn had regularly checked LoneStar's cockpit radar, while Titch and Martha had simply kept their eyes peeled as they rode out front on horseback.

'So, that's our season over,' said AntiGrav's pilot with a sigh.

'Is there anything we can do to help?' asked Titch.

The pilot shrugged and shook his head. 'I doubt it. We're just lucky that we got here in one piece,' he said, before pausing to consider Titch. 'Most Battle Championship contenders would be secretly pleased that a rival has had to pull out. It seems like you're one of a kind, kid. Your dad would have been proud.'

'My dad?' Titch's ears pricked up. 'Did you know him?'

'Sure did,' said the pilot. 'You look the spitting image of him.'

'I do?' For a moment, Titch looked taken aback. Long ago his father had been a Battle Champion, but he had gone missing one season. Titch had signed up as a competitor in the hope of finding out what had happened to him. 'Did you know him well?' he asked, desperate for clues.

'Only that he was a good man...' The pilot's voice trailed away, as if memories of the past had just caught up with him. 'Anyway, good luck,' he finished. 'You're hot news after your win last weekend. Everyone is talking about you!'

And with that, the AntiGrav crew turned away, leaving Titch lost in his thoughts.

•

Titch was up at first light the next morning. He headed straight for the Armoury, keen to begin preparations for LoneStar's first-round fight. Finn and Martha were already there, studying the draw that had been pinned to a board by the main gates.

'Do you want the good news?' asked Martha.

'Or the bad news?' Finn added. 'And when I say bad, I mean really bad.'

Titch looked at the list for himself. 'So, we're up against ShockWave.'

'I told you it was bad,' said Finn. 'That mech is so powerful it can cause earth tremors just by cranking up its energy unit to maximum. In the past, some opponents have been floored without ShockWave even touching them.'

Titch turned to Martha. 'So what's the good news?'

Martha smiled weakly. 'We've drawn the first fight of the day. So, there's little time to get nervous.'

'And that's the good news?' Titch turned his attention to LoneStar. The metal giant gleamed in the early sun. The cockpit was open, awaiting the pilot, and both the footplate and the steps were fully extended. Unlike many other Championship machines, Titch's mech had seen better days. Its battle scars were clear to see, especially the deep slash that crossed one side of the visor.

'Well, I'm not scared,' Titch finished. 'LoneStar is one of a kind.'

As he said this, another pilot appeared beside them to study the board. The man didn't look very friendly and sneered when he read the list. Then he faced Titch square on. 'Looks like we'll be seeing each other in the battleground this morning,' he said, towering over him. 'ShockWave is my mech. Together, we're gonna show you what it's like to fight the big boys!'

It was Finn who suggested that they head straight for the town's Scavenger Store where competitors could pick up bolt-on weapons to add to their mechs. According to Finn, Titch would need to spend all of the previous weekend's prize money on some first-class firepower now that LoneStar was set to go head to head with ShockWave.

'You'll be forced to take aim in what feels like earthquake conditions,' Finn warned, as they stood before a giant rack of bolt-on guns and rocket launchers. 'How about a DiveBomber?' He pointed at a snub-nosed weapon.

'It looks easy to fit,' said Martha. 'But how does it work?'

Finn grinned. 'Let's just say that if the ground is shaking under your feet, you don't need to worry about taking aim too accurately. You'll find out why when you fire it, but I think you'll be impressed.'

'It sounds like just what we need!' agreed Titch.

The storekeeper was standing behind the counter. He was reading the morning newspaper when the three friends crossed to pay. 'AntiGrav isn't the first mech to go missing out in Dismal Gorge,' he sighed. He closed the paper and looked up.

'Really?' said Titch. 'What do you mean?'

'We lost a Championship leader there many years ago,' said the storekeeper. 'But that's old news now.'

'My dad!' Titch cried. 'We know that he went missing! Surely, you must be talking about my dad?' Titch clung to the edge of the counter, eager for more information. Until now, he'd had no idea where his dad had last been seen. 'Do you know what happened to him?'

The storekeeper studied Titch for a moment. Then he nodded to himself, as if satisfied that the boy was genuine. 'People said that he died in a shoot-out there,' he told them. 'But the fact is that nobody knows for sure. No trace of him or his mech has ever been found.'

Titch thought about this for a moment. 'Well, one day I'll find out the truth,' he promised the storekeeper. 'For now, we'll focus on getting our mech battle-ready for the first round.' He glanced at Martha. Then he stepped back to let her order the weapon they had chosen for the fight.

'Are you OK?' asked Finn, placing a hand on Titch's shoulder.

'I'm fine,' said Titch bravely. 'Every clue that brings me closer to my dad also fires me up to do my best in the battleground.'

'Well, that's good to hear,' replied Finn. 'Because ShockWave is one of the toughest mechs you've had to face yet! We're going to need firepower — and a whole lot of it.'

3

The Battle Begins!

Later that morning, strapped inside LoneStar's cockpit, Titch turned the mech to face his opponent.

'All systems go,' said the onboard computer. Its voice was synthesised but sounded like a sergeant major. 'Good luck, Titch!'

'We don't need luck,' said Titch, speaking into his headset.

A camera was embedded in the mech's steel skull. The feed was projected onto the inside of Titch's visor. It allowed him to see what was going on outside. For a moment, Titch took in his surroundings. It was a warm, sticky day. A heat haze shimmered over the swamp. Bugs and dragonflies flitted this way and that, while the roar from the spectator stands was deafening. Titch was well aware that the crowds had begun chanting his name, but he couldn't let that go to his head. Not now.

His eyes narrowed as ShockWave appeared across the swamp. It was an electric-blue mech with a white lightning bolt painted across its chest. Sparks crackled and spat from its body as it moved.

'Your opponent is charging up for the fight,' reported the onboard computer. 'ShockWave's tactics can be explosive.'

'Hmm,' said Titch. 'Perhaps we will need luck on our side after all.'

Titch worked the levers in front of him until the two mechs had taken up their positions in the swamp. The grandstands were packed.

A blast from a horn marked the start

of the battle round. ShockWave made the first move by spreading its giant metal arms wide. At the same time, a low rumble began to build from deep inside the machine.

'Brace yourself,' said Titch's onboard computer. 'The mech is turning its power system to max.'

Very quickly, the rumble became so strong that the murky waters underneath them began to ripple. The mech itself appeared to be vibrating, but what really commanded Titch's attention was the arc of electricity bouncing from one steel palm to the other.

'What's going on?' Titch took LoneStar back a few steps to buy some time. 'I have a bad feeling about this!'

Titch reached for the dial that controlled the mech's cameras and zoomed in on his opponent's cockpit. Through the glass, he could see the pilot. The man was wrestling with the control sticks as if struggling to stop the mech from taking off like a rocket.

'We're about to find out what that mech can do,' reported the onboard computer. 'Tread sensors are reporting an unusual rise in ground movement. ShockWave is building up a massive charge of energy. As soon as that machine releases it, this whole swamp could blow sky-high!'

Titch didn't need to look at the control panel to see this for himself. The water surrounding his opponent had turned so choppy it looked like it was boiling.

'Arm the DiveBomber,' Titch said, raising his voice to be heard. The rumble was so loud now that it was hard for him to think straight. 'Let's show this mech that we're not just a sitting duck!'

Just as LoneStar swung the weapon into position, ShockWave made its move, clapping its great hands together.

Immediately, a blinding light filled Titch's camera feed. This was followed by a pressure blast so great it smashed Titch's mech off its feet. As LoneStar crashed into the swamp, it felt as if an earthquake was going off. Titch grappled with the control sticks, anxious to get the mech upright before the referee declared him the loser, but the swamp bed was shaking so badly he just couldn't find his balance.

'It's not too late to fire the DiveBomber!' the onboard computer said. 'Just aim it upwards and shoot!'

Without further thought, Titch popped the cap off the top of both control sticks and pressed the buttons underneath. With LoneStar on its back, the weapon fired up into the sky. As he did so, the camera feed switched to the view from the sleek missile now climbing into the air. The trouble was that it didn't seem to be aiming for anything more than the clouds.

'Is that it?' asked Titch, who had managed to get the mech up onto one knee by now. The missile appeared to be running out of power. It slowed and then tipped to begin the fall to earth. 'What a waste!'

'Guidance procedure is live,' the onboard computer told Titch. 'I've switched the sticks to weapon control. Time to bring that baby home!'

'What do you mean?' Titch was a little surprised to hear the computer talk in this way, but had no time to press for an explanation. He grabbed the control sticks and locked his sights on the projection on his visor. It continued to show the path of the DiveBomber, which was dropping towards ShockWave in the swamp below.

As the mech looked up, Titch eased the missile towards it. Sensing trouble, ShockWave began to wade rapidly through the water. Calmly, Titch followed the target, which grew in his sights as the missile closed in, and then BAM!

Quickly, Titch switched back to the view from LoneStar's head-mounted camera. He hadn't made a direct hit but the blast had clearly caused his opponent some damage. ShockWave staggered forwards, scorched from the blast. Titch zoomed in once more to see the pilot fighting to keep the mech under control.

'Now's our chance,' he said, raising LoneStar back onto its feet. 'This round belongs to us!'

Titch pushed his machine into a stride. As LoneStar splashed through the swamp, he pulled back one metal fist. The other pilot was struggling desperately to put ShockWave into retreat. With no time to lose, LoneStar delivered a final blow.

ShockWave didn't fall. Instead, the fighting machine stopped in its tracks, bowed its head and sagged its broad shoulders.

'You've shut down its power system!' cried LoneStar's onboard computer. 'We've won!'

Titch could hear the crowds go wild before he'd even climbed out of the cockpit. Once the footplate slid into place, he stepped out onto it and waved. Across the swamp, the stands were packed with people. Most were on their feet. Some even unfurled a banner with LoneStar emblazoned across it.

With no power left inside ShockWave, the other pilot was forced to push his cockpit doors apart in order to get out. He looked totally fed up, especially when a member of his crew paddled out in a canoe to inspect the damaged mech.

'What a win!' cried Titch and punched

the air. 'Round one belongs to us!'

The other pilot was also standing on the footplate of his mech now. He grasped the hand rail and glared at Titch. 'Don't be too confident, kid. You might have got lucky just then, but there are mech contenders lining up to put you back in your place.'

'Well we'll see about that!' Titch cried, his confidence sky-high. It was such a thrill to hear the crowd cheering for him. He turned to face the grandstands and narrowed his eyes in the hope of catching a glimpse of Martha and Finn. Instead, the figure he spotted hurrying down the central aisle of the stand took his breath away. He was wearing a skunk-skin hat and a tasselled leather trench coat. Titch couldn't mistake that outfit, because he knew there was only one man who wore it. 'Wyatt Thorne?' he breathed.

The last time he came face to face with the notorious outlaw, Titch had been training to become a Championship contender at Mech Academy. Thorne had mounted a raid in a bid to steal some trainer mechs. Fortunately, Titch and his friends had foiled him, but Wyatt Thorne was still at large.

Titch looked down at the footplate for just a moment, struggling to think straight. That man was trouble, that was for sure.

But when Titch looked back up again, the figure on the stands was nowhere to be seen.

● ● ●

4
Malfunction Mayhem

LoneStar had suffered very little damage in its first-round fight. When Titch piloted the mech back to the Armoury, Martha had just one suggestion.

'We need a pressure hose,' she said. 'This machine smells swampy and needs a major wash down! If there's one thing I can't stand, it's a messy mech!'

Titch grinned and looked up at the metal giant. Martha was right. Long strands of pondweed were clinging to LoneStar. Even so, the machine still looked perfect in his eyes. 'I'm beginning to think that nobody can beat us,' he said, as Finn prepared to climb the steps and reset the controls for the next round.

'Don't get too confident.' Finn grinned. 'That's when mistakes are made.'

'Finn's right,' Martha added. 'You've done well, but we've got a long way to go in this Championship season.'

'Nah. You guys are losing your nerve,' said Titch, waving away their words of warning. 'Just you wait and see! Whatever round two brings, I'll be ready!'

•

Once LoneStar had been cleaned, the three friends spent a few hours watching the other mechs take part in their competing rounds. One fight in particular caught their attention. It was between SprintJet and HoverTank. The winner would fight Titch and LoneStar tomorrow.

Titch, however, chose not to stick around for the whole battle. 'I'll see you later, guys,' he said. 'I'm off for an afternoon's fishing.'

'But don't you want to stick around to see who wins?' asked Martha.

'We might pick up some fighing tips,' Finn added, but Titch had made up his mind. As he left, the twins looked at each other and shrugged. It seemed surprising, but perhaps he needed some time out.

The fight proved to be a spectacular clash. Both mechs made full use of their abilities to soar across the surface of the swamp while trading shots and blows. By the time Titch returned to the guesthouse at dusk, clutching a brace of catfish he had caught to barbeque, the twins had begun to worry about him.

'If you want to be a Battle Champion,' said Martha, 'you need to live and breathe the sport.'

'I know that,' Titch sighed. 'I've won every one of my Battle Championship rounds so far.

'Even so, you should've stayed to watch the fight,' Finn joined in. 'HoverTank was the favourite to win, but SprintJet put up an epic fight. That machine was super-fast. Half the time, HoverTank had no idea where his opponent was located on the battleground. The final blow made the ground shake!'

'Well, I'm not scared of SprintJet,' said Titch, who was a little disappointed that the twins hadn't first complimented him on his catch. 'I needed some time off to think over what I learned about my father. Finding out what happened to him is really important to me, guys. Right now I'm so tired that all I need to be ready for round two is a hot meal and good night's sleep.'

Martha pressed her lips together. She wished that she could be so confident. Titch really should have stuck around to take in every tiny detail of the last battle round. Still, she guessed he knew what he was doing. 'OK,' she said with a sigh, and looked at the catfish. 'Let's get those cooking on the barbeque. The sooner we eat and get some sleep, the better.'

•

Before turning in for the night, the three friends sat out on the porch once more. Finn was keen to brief Titch on some of the small changes he had made to LoneStar's battleground mapping system. He knew that such minor adjustments could have a big impact on the fight, as did his sister. Between them, they had worked hard to make sure that the mech was in perfect fighting form.

'It's vital if you want to keep track of your opponent,' Finn told Titch. I've upgraded the overhead view to make it easier for you to see what's going on at a glance. Basically, you can now lock onto your enemy,Titch? Are you listening?'

'What's that noise?' Titch sat forward

in his chair. He raised one hand to signal to the twins to stay quiet. 'There's something out there.'

'All I hear is mosquitoes buzzing,' said Martha and promptly slapped the side of her neck. 'Gotcha!'

'It's not a mosquito,' whispered Titch, who rose from his chair. 'It sounds like it's coming from the Armoury!'

This time, the twins listened carefully. That area was out of bounds from sundown to sunrise. It was also heavily guarded, as Finn reminded Titch, so it was strange to hear noises.

'It's probably an alligator prowling the perimeter,' said Finn. 'After last time, I don't think it would be a good idea to go looking.'

'Finn's right, Titch,' said Martha, still rubbing her neck where the mosquito had bitten her. 'The best thing we can do right now is head inside, shut the door against the bugs and get some shut-eye!'

Overnight, a thick mist settled over the swampland. It hung over the surface of the water in slashed veils. Still, at first light it didn't stop the crowds from flocking to the stands for what would be the second knockout round of the weekend.

'I have a good feeling about this fight,' said Titch as he guided LoneStar from the Armoury.

'I don't think you'll find it as easy as yesterday's round,' warned the onboard computer. 'SprintJet has speed on his side. He's also known to spring a surprise. Just be careful out there, Titch.'

Titch grinned and pushed the control sticks forward. 'If anyone needs to watch out,' he said, 'it's SprintJet.'

Finn and Martha looked at each other. They both seemed a little concerned.

That morning, Titch and LoneStar were the

first to arrive in the battleground.

To a roar from the crowd, they waded through the water. Knowing that his opponent was equipped to glide over the surface of the swamp, using hovercraft technology, Titch had chosen to arm LoneStar with the only weapon he believed would bring it down – the SkyPunch! Titch hadn't used it before, but as soon as

Martha had bolted it onto the mech's arm, he had felt sure that it would do the job. The device was simple. It fired a supercharged blast of air at its opponent that could knock a hovering mech off-course. If they could hit SprintJet from the side and then pounce when the mech was attempting to recover, round two would be over in no time at all!

'One minute until battle begins,' the onboard computer reported. No sign of another mech on our radar.'

Titch glanced at the screen. According to LoneStar's position, they were close to the creeks and backwoods at the far end of the swamp. 'Let's get into position over there,' he suggested, gesturing at a small island of hardwood trees and creepers. 'It'll give us cover if we come under early fire.'

When a horn sounded, marking the start of the battle round, Titch was feeling even more upbeat about his chances –

until his radar showed the arrival of his opponent.

'Wow!' he said with a whistle as a red dot began to circle the swamp. 'That mech is quick!'

'That's what everybody has been saying!' replied the onboard computer. 'So, what's the strategy, Titch?'

'Strategy?' Titch switched his view from radar to real time. As he did so, SprintJet whooshed by the island so fast that it caused the trees to sway and shake. Titch locked the camera view onto the speeding mech and was taken aback by what he saw. SprintJet had a massive engine moulded to its back and wings that spread wide as it raced over the surface of the swamp. Judging by the way the mech came back around, the pilot inside had just located its quarry.

'Bring out the SkyPunch!' Titch commanded, preparing to unleash the weapon's true power. His finger found the trigger but his eyes remained locked on his opponent as it turned to speed past. Titch timed his attack to perfection. As soon as SprintJet was within his line of sight he squeezed the trigger and nothing. 'What's wrong?' he asked, pressing the trigger again. 'What's happening? Why

isn't it working?'

'We have a malfunction,' replied the onboard computer. 'I've just run an auto-repair sweep, but it doesn't seem to be the system software.'

Titch watched his opponent sweeping back around. All of a sudden, he didn't feel so confident.'If it isn't the software,' he

said, 'then what's the problem?'

'It appears to be a hardware issue,' the onboard computer replied after a moment. 'Either the SkyPunch isn't bolted on properly or something has broken off.'

In desperation, Titch tried the trigger one more time and cried out angrily when it failed to fire the weapon. After all that lecturing from Martha about being prepared, it seemed as if the mechanic was the one who'd gone and let them down.

'This could be the end of our weekend,' Titch groaned, just as SprintJet unleashed a round of explosive needles from the NailStormer guns fitted under its wings. 'But we're not going down without a fight!'

● ● ●

5

Team Fireworks

The battle round was long and hard. With no weapons to call upon, all Titch could rely on were his quick wits. And faced with an airborne mech, that was no easy task. Within minutes, SprintJet had landed a number of hits on LoneStar. Luckily, Titch had managed to dodge the worst of the NailStormer needles. Even so, his mech was badly damaged. As SprintJet raced away from its latest attack, preparing to come round from a different angle to repeat the onslaught, Titch retreated for the creeks.

'Your fans will think you're running away,' said the onboard computer. 'Just listen to them jeering. Is this wise?'

Titch was well aware of the boos and whistles coming from the stands. He was also focused on the fact that his opponent was closing in behind.

'What choice do I have?' he asked through gritted teeth. 'This is about survival!'

With the control sticks pushed as far forward as they would go, LoneStar thundered through the murky shallows. The creek itself was flanked by steep banks. It gave Titch an idea. There was a strong chance it wouldn't work, but what choice did he have?

'Pinpoint the narrowest section of the creek!' he commanded the onboard computer. 'Bring it up on the battlemap!'

At once, a digital crosshair floated onto the screen and then locked onto a point some way ahead.

'It's barely wide enough for us to pass through,' warned the computer.

'Perfect!' cried Titch as the mech continued to splash through the shallows. 'Let's push on!'

SprintJet was still out in the swamp, but now it turned and began to rocket after Titch inside his mech. The rival machine moved so low and so quick that it left a trail of choppy water behind it.

'Twenty metres to the narrowest point,' said the computer and began to count down. 'This is going to be a tight squeeze!'

Titch focused on the camera feed and scrunched his eyes tight. As they hurtled towards the gap, he put his plan into action. First he threw LoneStar into a headlong dive. The machine passed between the two walls of rock, scraping the sides in a spray of sparks. Slamming the control sticks back, Titch managed to bring the mech's feet down into the water before spinning around to watch his opponent.

'If this doesn't work, we're in trouble!'

he declared.

From the distance, Titch could see that SprintJet was in hot pursuit. The mech was flying at such a rate that there would be no chance of stopping before it reached the gap. With such a huge wingspan, it was also clear that the mech wasn't going to pass through like LoneStar. The pilot must have realised that for himself because, with seconds to spare, he ejected high into the air...

KABOOM!

SprintJet connected with the creek walls with such force that both wings sheared off into the water.

'We did it!' cried the onboard computer as the rival pilot's parachute opened up high overhead. 'No, wait!'

Titch had already spotted the danger. SprintJet's torso was still hurtling towards them. Instead of being an airborne fighting machine, the mech was little more than an

unmanned missile heading straight at them!

'There's only one thing for it!' cried Titch, before grabbing the control sticks and throwing LoneStar flat into the water.

What was left of SprintJet whizzed over them, before catching the surface of the creek and then cartwheeling off into the trees.

•

For the second time that weekend, LoneStar returned to the Armoury covered in weed from the swamp. Despite winning the round, the mech had also picked up more than a few dents and scratches!

'Yeew!' cried Martha, as the footplate slid out and the steps unfolded to the ground. 'Could you have brought it back any filthier?' She watched the telescopic support struts drop into place underneath and then shook her head at Titch when he climbed out of the cockpit. 'Of course I'm thrilled that you're through to the final round, but what a mess!'

'Not as much of a mess as SprintJet,' said Titch, as the recovery truck hauled the tangled remains of his opponent back to the waiting crew. The pilot was trudging along behind, soaked to the skin, with his ejector parachute bundled in his arms. 'But that could've been LoneStar, Martha. Our weapon didn't work when I needed it most! You couldn't have fitted it properly. What happened?'

Martha looked shocked as Titch made his way down the steps. 'But the mech was definitely battle-ready,' she said. 'I checked everything before supper last night!'

'Then you didn't check hard enough!'

'What's the problem?' Just at that moment, Finn appeared as Martha and Titch continued to exchange cross words. 'Calm down, guys! We're a team, remember?'

'Some team!' Titch spat back. 'If I can't even trust my engineer to do a simple job then we might as well quit the Championship trail right now!'

'Titch!' Finn looked shocked. 'That's no way to speak to Martha. You might've had a hard time out there, but I'm sure it's not her fault!'

'OK, enough!' said Martha, blinking back tears. 'If Titch feels I've let him down then I shouldn't be here any more.' She began to back away. Then, before Finn could respond, Martha turned and ran.

'Marvellous!' said Finn crossly and faced Titch once more. 'If my sister has just quit, then I'm out too!'

● ● ●

6
The Missing Mechanic

Alone with his thoughts, it wasn't long before Titch felt bad. Really bad. Even if Martha had made a mistake when preparing LoneStar for battle, Finn was right. She wouldn't have done it on purpose and she certainly hadn't deserved to be snapped at like that.

'I've been an idiot,' he said out loud, having climbed back into the cockpit for some space and time to think.

As if in response, several lights on the control panel began to blink.

'Well if it's any help, I've just checked my memory records from yesterday,' said the onboard computer. 'They show that

Martha fitted the weapon perfectly. She even made sure all systems, including me, were properly powered down before nightfall, as per Championship rules.'

'Now that just makes me feel even worse!' Titch sat back in his seat and sighed. He stared out across the Armoury through the open cockpit hatch. Rival mechs stood all around, gleaming in the sun like giant statues. Down at ground level, their crews worked hard to prepare them for the next round.

'Without Martha and Finn we're finished!' muttered Titch.

'Can I offer you some advice?' said the onboard computer. 'A good pilot should learn from his mistakes. It isn't too late to apologise, Titch. That's if Martha and Finn haven't already left town.'

Titch watched another pilot prepare to climb into his mech. Clutching his helmet under one arm, he looked calm and collected. It was just how Titch needed to feel if he stood a chance in that afternoon's final round.

'Don't go anywhere,' he told the onboard computer as he prepared to climb out of the cockpit. 'I'll be right back. Hopefully my friends will be with me.'

•

At the guesthouse, Titch found Finn folding the last of his clothes into his kit bag. The door to his room was open, but Titch still knocked to gain his attention.

'If you've come here to be rude and grumpy again, then save your breath,' said Finn. 'It's been brilliant riding the Battle Championship trail with you, Titch, but I've had enough. Lately you've changed. You're a great mech pilot — and behind every great pilot is a rock-solid team. It's just you seem to have forgotten that.'

'I know, I know,' said Titch, looking down at the floor. 'I can't help it. Every time

I come across a clue about my dad, I feel all the more determined to find out what happened to him. It's making me tense, but I shouldn't have taken it out on Martha and you. I'm sorry, Finn. I was out of order.'

Finn nodded, like he understood. 'Your father would be proud of what you're doing, you know.'

'Maybe.' Titch smiled. 'But I don't think he'd be very proud of the way I spoke to my friends. For the time being, I need to focus on being the best mech pilot in town,' he said. 'And that means working closely with you both to prepare for the third and final round.'

Now Finn beamed broadly. 'We'd better find Martha and tell her the good news,' he said. 'She's probably packing in her room.'

'Let's go right now,' said Titch. 'I need to say a very big sorry to her, too.'

The pair headed down the guesthouse corridor, smiling and joking with one another. Outside Martha's room, Titch raised his hand to knock. Then he realised the door was slightly open.

'Hello?' said Finn. 'Are you there, sis?' Titch pushed the door back. 'Her stuff is still here,' he said, looking around. 'But there's no sign of Martha.'

'I followed her back to the guesthouse earlier,' said Finn. 'She told me she was just going to lie down and think about things for a while.'

It was then that Titch noticed a scratch on the door frame. 'Look at this,' he said, kneeling down for a closer look. 'It looks like someone has tried to cling on with their fingertips but been prised away!'

Titch was only joking, but Finn looked concerned for a moment. Having checked it out for himself, he stepped back and shrugged.

'She's probably just gone for a walk to clear her head,' he said. 'Why don't we head back to the Armoury and start work on LoneStar? We can fine-tune the systems until Martha shows up. I'm sure once you've cleared the air with her she'll put her heart and soul into making sure that mech is packing a punch!'

•

It took some time for Finn and Titch to get back to LoneStar. Not only did the spectators pack out the grandstands to

watch each fight, but many crowded at the fencing around the Armoury for a glimpse of the crews at work on their mechs. Finn and Titch took a while to squeeze their way through to the main gate. Once they had cleared the security check, they strolled towards their giant machine.

'I get a buzz every time I set eyes on LoneStar,' said Titch as they climbed the steps to the cockpit.

'Me too,' said Finn, who followed behind. 'Our mech might have seen better days, but it's a part of the team just like the rest of us.'

Titch drew breath to agree, only to stop suddenly on reaching the footplate at the top of the steps.

'What's this?' He reached out and tore off a sheet of paper taped to the cockpit door. 'Oh, no,' he whispered, and then showed it to Finn, slowly reading the words. 'If you want Martha back safe and sound, bring the prize money you've earned so far to Dismal Gorge by sundown.' The two boys exchanged a look of shock and concern.

'So she's been kidnapped!' said Titch.

'But who would do that?' asked Finn.

Titch narrowed his eyes, thinking hard. Then he spun around and opened the cockpit doors. 'I don't know, but there might just be a way that we can find out.' He reached in to activate the onboard computer.

'What's up?' asked the synthesised voice.

'I need you to replay all the footage from the cockpit monitor for the last hour,' said Titch, gesturing at the camera mounted to a bracket behind the pilot's seat. 'Play it on fast forward. We haven't got time to waste!'

Finn leaned in alongside Titch as a side monitor came alive. It showed a shot through the smoked-glass cockpit window. Outside, clouds drifted across the sky at treble speed as the onboard computer spooled through the footage. Then, seemingly out of nowhere, a figure popped up on the footplate.

'Stop there!' said Finn. 'Now play it at half speed and zoom in on that face!'

Titch squinted. It was hard to make out who they were watching at first, but then Titch took in the grizzled features and drooping moustache of a familiar figure. There was only one man he knew who wore a skunk skin and a tasselled leather trench coat. 'Wyatt Thorpe,' he breathed.

Titch watched the footage of the figure scuttling back down the steps and then glanced over his shoulder. Across town, over in the swampland battleground, the grandstand was filled to the brim. It was too far away to spot individual faces, but he remembered thinking he had seen the same person there the day before – an outlaw who was never a welcome sight.

'Wyatt Thorne was here yesterday,' said Titch calmly. 'I wasn't sure it was him at the time, but now I've seen this footage I'm certain.'

'That bandit is in town?' Finn sucked in his breath. 'He's trouble!'

Titch didn't need to remind Finn that he was talking about a man in charge of a band of outlaws called the Wired Bunch, and their eight-legged mechs. Wyatt and his band prowled the badlands, living on the wrong side of the law.

'But what would Wyatt Thorne want with Martha?' Finn asked, puzzled. 'It can't just be about the money? He must know we've been spending it on new weapons to get us through the Championship.'

'I foiled Wyatt's raid on the Mech Academy,' Titch reminded him.

'Then he's also after revenge?' asked Finn.

'I don't know.' Titch crumpled up the note in his fist.' But if Thorne is behind this ransom demand, then Martha is in big trouble!'

'So what can we do?' asked Finn.

'There's only one thing for it,' said Titch, inviting Finn to clamber into the cockpit. 'Take us to Dismal Gorge!'

7

Dismal Gorge

With no time to saddle up a horse, Titch stayed out on the footplate. As soon as the automatic steps folded up, Finn steered LoneStar out of the Armoury. The main street was crowded, but nobody could ignore the thunderous footfalls of a walking machine that was as high as a grain store. Titch grasped the handrail and looked out over the rooftops. Once they were clear of Crawfish Creek and on the trail that would take them out of the swamplands, Finn pushed the mech into a sprint.

'Go as fast as you can!' cried Titch, who found himself being thrown about like a rider at a rodeo. 'I can handle it!'

'I hope so,' replied Finn, addressing him through a speaker above the cockpit hatch. 'For Martha's sake, we need to get there as fast as we can!'

•

Dismal Gorge lived up to its name. Here, the trail passed between two looming walls of rock. Steep paths, caves and jagged outcrops provided plenty of hiding places for anyone hoping to stage an ambush. It was also horribly quiet, as Titch discovered having pulled LoneStar to a halt midway through.

'Anything on the radar?' he asked, when Finn opened up the cockpit and stepped out to join him.

'Every now and then a red dot lights up and then melts away.' Finn looked up and around. 'I have a feeling we're not alone out here.'

The mech had stopped beneath a rocky arch that spanned the gorge. Titch studied it for a moment. 'I have an idea,' he said, pointing at the arch. 'First I'll need LoneStar to lift me up there.'

'No problem,' Finn replied, and climbed back inside the cockpit. 'Just watch your back!'

A moment later, having climbed onto the mech's giant metal palm, Titch rose up towards the arch. As he drew level, he saw coils of rope. It was clearly a spot where bandits lay in wait. Titch unclipped his walkie-talkie and spoke into the mouthpiece. 'I'm guessing this is where they drop down on their quarry,' he whispered. 'Move LoneStar into the shadows while I investigate. I don't want to come back and find that you've gone missing, too!'

'Understood,' replied Finn. 'Be safe out there.'

Titch climbed off the mech and crouched low. On one side of the gorge, way out in the distance, he could see a twist of smoke rising into the sky. 'There's a campfire burning,' he radioed back to Finn. 'Give me ten minutes. If I'm not back in that time, get back to Crawfish Creek and sound the alarm.'

'Sure thing,' said Finn.

Titch moved quick and low through the scrub, heading away from Dismal Gorge. Cacti studded the ground and vultures circled overhead. He was in the badlands. That was clear. The kind of place the Battle Championship organisers warned competitors to avoid. As he scurried towards the smoke, he could hear the crackle of a campfire, as well as laughing and jeering. Titch dashed from one hiding place to the next, until he found himself looking down at a clearing. He recognised the men straightaway. Quietly, he reached for his walkie-talkie.

'It's the Wired Bunch,' he whispered.

'Their spider mechs are surrounding the camp. It could be that they've got something valuable with them that they're trying to protect.'

'Understood. Any sign of Martha?' asked Finn.

'I'm going to take a closer look,' replied Titch.

Moving off quickly and quietly, Titch used every shadow and rock to hide behind as he made his way into the camp. Several outlaws were patrolling the perimeter formed by the spider mechs. He waited for the two men to pass one another before slipping under the body of the closest eight-legged machine. There, flat on his belly in the dirt, he scanned the camp for any sign of Martha. She would be hard to miss among so many unshaven, weather-beaten bandits. Even so, it quickly became clear to Titch that she wasn't a part of the camp. Wyatt Thorne was also nowhere to be seen, he realised, and that's when he began to get seriously worried.

'What have you done with her?' he whispered, shaking his head in frustration.

Titch was just about to crawl back out from under the spider mech when a sound stopped him in his tracks. It was coming from inside the cockpit of the machine itself – and sounded a lot like a girl sobbing. He glanced up, and then across at the two patrolling bandits. If he acted quickly, there was a chance he could get inside the machine to investigate before they came back around. Without further thought, Titch scrambled into the open and scaled the rungs up the side of the mech. The hatch was bolted from the outside. He hauled it back and pulled on the handle, and then gasped at the tear-streaked face peering up at him.

'Martha!'

'You shouldn't have come!' she whispered,

looking both relieved and terrified. 'These guys are dangerous!'

Titch glanced across at the campfire. At any moment, one of them could turn around and spot him. 'Do you know how to hotwire a mech?'

'Sure I do,' she replied. 'The starter system can be overridden from a panel at the back.'

'Then let's do it,' Titch whispered, extending a hand to help her out.

By now, the guards on patrol were on the point of coming back around. Titch hauled Martha from her makeshift prison. Together, they scrambled off the mech and into the shadows.

'It's right here,' she whispered, pulling at a metal flap on the body of the great crawling machine.

'Hurry!' Titch glanced over his shoulder. He could hear the two guards crunching through the dirt.

The open flap revealed a tangle of wires. Carefully, Martha eased out a green and a red one. She then touched the ends together. With a spark and a crackle, the mech's engine coughed into life.

'Hey! You kids! What do you think you're playing at?'

Titch wheeled around to see the two guards thundering towards them. The chatter around the campfire had turned to cries of surprise.

'The Wired Bunch are onto us!' he cried, urging Martha to scale the rungs. 'Get back inside the cockpit as quickly as you can!'

Titch followed his friend up. As he raced to the top of the mech, one of the guards rushed towards him. He grabbed at Titch's ankle. In desperation, Titch kicked him away before climbing the last rungs and diving through the hatch.

'Spin it shut from the inside,' he

instructed Martha, while climbing into the pilot's seat. 'It may be a squeeze for two in here, but it's better than being on the outside right now!'

Titch fired up the spider mech's camera feed. It showed a scene of chaos, with bandits running in every direction. Some had thrown themselves onto the spider mech, only to tumble away when Titch

snapped the machine up onto its eight legs. Twisting the control sticks, the machine span around. It sent another bandit flying, who could do nothing but watch from the dirt as the mech began to crawl from the clearing.

'This thing is slow!' cried Martha, bunched up behind the pilot's seat. 'Let me see if I can do something about that.' She reached across the cockpit and began to jab at a series of buttons on a control panel.

The spider mech lurched to one side, as if it had lost its footing, before coming to an unexpected halt.

'Is there a problem?' asked Titch, wheeling around in his seat.

'Hold on.' Martha flicked a switch and then pressed the buttons again. This time, the mech levelled up and moved on at double speed. 'Sorry about that,' she said with a grin. 'I'm not that familiar with these machines.'

'What happened to you?' asked Titch, as the sound of bullets could be heard striking the mech's armoured body.

'Wyatt Thorne snatched me from my room,' said Martha. 'He threw me over his shoulder and took great delight in telling me how he'd disabled LoneStar's weapon system.'

Titch glanced at Martha, feeling bad to hear that Wyatt had confessed to the sabotage. He drew breath to apologise to Martha for even thinking she could've messed up, only to gasp as another bullet bounced off the back of the mech. Titch swivelled the camera view, which showed a trail of spider mechs scuttling out in pursuit. 'Time to call the cavalry!' he said and snatched the walkie-talkie from his belt. 'Finn, I'm on my way back with Martha, but the Wired Bunch are in pursuit!'

'I can see you on the radar,' Finn

replied. 'What can I do? The SkyPunch is out of action.'

'Not for much longer!' said Martha, leaning forward to be heard. 'Finn, do you see a key underneath the trigger panel?'

'Got it,' replied Finn.

'Give it a twist. It'll route the weapon system to core power. Doesn't matter what wires Wyatt might've cut, the SkyPunch will be online again.'

Titch grinned at Martha. 'It's good to have you back onboard,' he said, before speaking to her brother. 'Fire at will, Finn. We need your help out here!'

'I got your backs, guys! LoneStar and I won't let you down!'

Titch switched the camera view to face the front once more. By now they were moving at speed across the scrubland. Just then, from the horizon up ahead, a missile climbed into the sky. It left a column of smoke behind that buckled in the breeze.

'Here comes the SkyPunch!' said Titch, as the missile began to tip towards the earth once more. 'I hope Finn has a steady hand now he's guiding that to the target.'

For a moment, both Titch and Martha watched in silence as the missile sailed out of the sky. When it whistled over their machine, Titch swivelled the camera to follow it. Behind them, the spider mechs who had been giving chase were busy scattering far and wide.

'No need for a direct hit,' Titch instructed Finn over the walkie-talkie. 'Just scare them up so they leave us alone.'

'Understood,' said Finn.

A split second later, the missile hit the ground. The explosion was intense. It threw up a big fireball, causing several spider mechs to tumble. Finn had carried out the hit to perfection.

'They're heading back to camp,' cried Titch, smiling to himself as the machines picked themselves up and began to crawl away. 'You did it, Finn!'

'We all played a part,' replied the test pilot. 'We're a team, remember?'

Titch smiled to himself. He drew breath to agree, only for Martha to gasp and point at the radar.

'Another missile has just been launched from Dismal Gorge! It's locked onto us!'

Titch span around in his seat to check

the radar. Martha was right.

'Finn, is that you?' he cried.

'Negative!' replied Finn. 'LoneStar's weapon system is back in safe mode.'

'Here it comes!' gasped Titch, his eyes locked on the screen. Unlike the SkyPunch, the missile that sprang into view didn't lift high into the air. Instead, it soared out of the gorge and then corkscrewed low across the scrubland towards them.

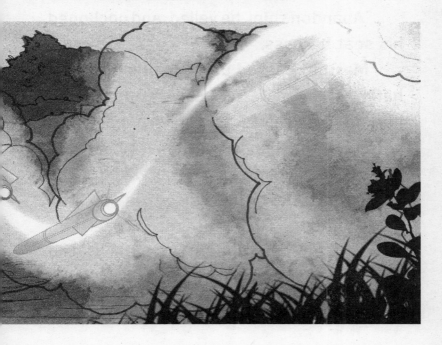

'That's an AirScythe,' said Martha. 'Those missiles are only licensed for use in the Battle Championship! Once they lock onto their target there's no escape!'

'What does it do?' asked Titch.

'It doesn't carry explosives, but trust me, it'll finish off this mech!'

Titch grabbed the control sticks, but by then even he could see that any attempt to move the spider mech would be pointless.

'Abandon ship!' he yelled, and unclipped his seat harness.

Martha reached up and spun open the hatch. The pair scrambled out before hurling themselves to the ground. Titch softened the impact with a roll, as did Martha. Behind them, with a whistle, the low-flying AirScythe closed in on the spider mech. Titch turned to see two curved steel bars snap out of the casing on each side. It meant that when the missile passed under the mech's body, the bars made contact with its front legs. With a groan as the metal limbs buckled, the machine slumped to the ground.

'Wow! Titch exclaimed after a moment, as he and Martha picked themselves up and brushed the dirt from their clothes. 'I'm glad nobody's ever fired one of those at LoneStar!'

'It's a lethal weapon for sure,' said Martha, who studied the wrecked mech in front of her. 'But who could've fired it?'

'I think we both know the answer to that,' said Titch. 'We might've escaped from the Wired Bunch, but clearly Wyatt Thorne isn't going to give up without a fight. He must be desperate to use those sorts of tactics. Come on, let's head back to LoneStar. This Spider Mech is useless to us now.'

● ● ●

8
Showdown!

On the trail back to Crawfish Creek, Titch and Martha rode out on the footplate. They kept watch for any sign of an ambush, but the only thing to spring from the bushes were birds startled by the giant fighting machine.

'Nothing to report on the radar,' said Finn from inside LoneStar's cockpit. 'If Wyatt Thorne was behind that missile strike, then he's nowhere to be seen now.'

'What's more,' said Martha, glancing at her wristwatch, 'we're in time to take part in the final round.'

'Awesome!' Titch grinned, just as the tiled rooftops of Crawfish Creek appeared behind the trees. 'It's good to go into battle knowing that we're a team again!'

•

The three friends headed directly for the Armoury. There, they hurried down LoneStar's automatic steps to check the leader board. It revealed not just one surprise but two.

'You were supposed to fight a mech called MashCrash, but that's been cancelled.' Martha read the details underneath the posting. Then she turned to relay it to Titch. 'Apparently MashCrash has developed a critical fault with its target lock-on system. The mechanic has tried to fix it but the mech keeps attacking itself. The team has decided to retire their machine for its own safety.'

'So, does that mean we've come out top again this weekend?' asked Finn. Martha shook her head. 'Another mech is taking MashCrash's place. It's been agreed by the organisers because the show must go on.'

'That's cool,' said Titch. 'Who?'

Martha raised one eyebrow and smiled. 'It seems we were not alone in coming back from the badlands. Do you remember what we heard at the start of the competition – about the mech that had gone missing?' Finn and Titch glanced at one another. 'Do you mean AntiGrav?'

'I sure do,' chuckled Martha. 'Somehow, that mech is back in town, and the organisers have given the crew permission to fight in the final round. Apparently they want to show the bandits that nothing can disrupt the Championship. Not even a mech hijack! It's a show of strength and every crew is backing it.'

'Amazing,' said Finn. 'Everyone believed AntiGrav would've been broken down for parts and sold on the border by now.'

'Well, apparently not,' said Martha.

'We'd better make sure LoneStar is in fighting form, because AntiGrav can literally turn your world upside down!'

•

For the final round of the Battle Championship weekend, both the grandstands and the shores of the swamp were packed. People had climbed trees to witness the two metal gladiators square up to one another, and a great cheer went up when the starter horn sounded.

'There's no sign of AntiGrav yet,' said Titch, who had stationed LoneStar in the very centre of the swamp. He turned the mech full circle, but saw nothing except a pelican flapping low across the water.

'I suggest you place your finger on the trigger just in case,' said the onboard computer. 'Our opponent is the master of surprise.'

Titch stared at the camera feed projected on his visor. A moment later, he spotted a disturbance on the surface of the swamp some distance away. 'What's that?' he asked himself, as a wave shaped like a wedge moved towards them.

'It's too big to be an alligator,' the onboard computer reported.

Without further thought, Titch found the trigger buttons on top of the control sticks. Finn had used the last SkyPunch missile to frighten off the Wired Bunch. As a result, Martha had decided to arm LoneStar with Titch's favourite form of firepower. The NailStormer fired a cloud of steel-tipped needles that each carried an explosive charge. It wasn't the most sophisticated weapon available from the Scavenger Store, but Titch had proved in the past that he could put it to good use.

'Here it comes,' warned the onboard computer, as the wave rose all of a sudden and the crown of the mech's head emerged from the swamp.

'Bring it on!' Titch prepared LoneStar to make the first move. His system monitor showed that everything was working perfectly, thanks to Martha.

As his opponent continued to rise out of the swamp, Titch made a split-second decision. Rather than fire off a round of needles, he decided to meet his opponent head on. If he could body-slam his opponent back into the water before pulling the trigger, victory would be in his sights.

Thinking of the win, Titch threw both control sticks forward. With a jolt, LoneStar hurled itself at AntiGrav. But just as Titch spread the mech's arms wide, the strangest thing happened. LoneStar simply came to a halt in mid-air, as if it had hit an invisible wall. Stopped dead in its tracks, the mech then belly-flopped straight down into the swamp.

'Not again!' moaned the onboard

computer as Titch struggled to lift the weed-strewn mech back onto its feet.

AntiGrav continued to rise out of the swamp. It was double the size of LoneStar and also twice as wide. As the machine gained height, Titch realised it was revolving from the waist down. In fact, its legs were spinning around at such a speed that they quickly became a blur. What's more, when AntiGrav began to move backwards, in order to take aim at LoneStar, it appeared to be floating over the surface of the water.

'How is it doing that?' asked Titch.

'It's a gyroscopic device,' the onboard computer explained. 'Not only can it defy gravity, but it's also created a powerful force-field. Looking at the data we're picking up, it appears to be impossible to penetrate.'

'Impossible?' Titch sounded concerned as his opponent began to turn in a wide circle around him.

'The mech is basically untouchable,' continued the computer. 'Unless you can hit the valve just above the cockpit. It's a power vent, like a pressure release in the force-field, and the only part of the machine that's vulnerable to attack.'

Titch was listening, while at the same time making sure that LoneStar stayed

moving. He didn't want to be a sitting target as his opponent took aim. Despite what the onboard computer had told him, he fired off a volley from the NailStormer. The needles glowed as they sailed through the air, only to explode one by one just a second before reaching the target. It was then that AntiGrav responded by firing his weapon. When the missile began spiralling towards him, Titch recognised it straight away.

'That's an AirScythe!'

'Correct,' said the onboard computer. 'And some evasive action would be good right now!'

It was the same missile Titch had faced earlier, out in the badlands, when he and Martha were holed up in the Spider Mech. This time, Titch had no intention of abandoning his mech. Knowing that he couldn't dodge or outrun the AirScythe, Titch pushed down on the control sticks.

He had just one plan in mind. Just as the curved bars sprung from each side of the missile, Titch hauled up both sticks. With a jolt, LoneStar sprung into the air. For a moment, it looked as if Titch had cleared the missile. Then a sickening crunch, together with a warning alarm inside the cockpit, told him he hadn't been completely successful.

'We've suffered a blow,' reported the onboard computer. 'LoneStar's left foot isn't responding. Worse still, we're taking on water down there!'

'This battle has only just begun!' cried Titch. He thrust the control sticks forward, only the mech didn't respond as he expected. Instead of moving out of range at speed, in case AntiGrav fired again, the machine stumbled and then splashed face first into the swamp.

Titch saw it coming on the camera. The surface of the water rushed towards them, and then suddenly Titch was looking out at fishes in the murk. Water rushed in through some of the rivets that held the cockpit hatch in place, which drenched Titch in his seat.

'Now we've lost balance auto correction,' the onboard computer said. 'Short circuits caused by flood damage.'

'I have to get a shot at that valve,' said Titch, aware that he had just one means of felling his opponent. 'Now where is AntiGrav?'

• • •

9
On Target

With the muscles in his arms straining, Titch hauled LoneStar back onto its feet. Water flowed from the mech's torso. The camera lens took a moment to clear. That's when Titch spotted his quarry. AntiGrav was still hovering over the water, but appeared to be focused on showing off to the crowds. Its lower limbs were spinning so fast it had caused the water to form a whirlpool. At the same time, the mech had raised both arms and clasped its hands above its head.

'Does the pilot think he's won?' asked the on-board computer.

'We took a big hit,' agreed Titch, and

activated the target system. 'But we're not done yet.'

This time, Titch magnified the target. It meant that when AntiGrav turned and saw that LoneStar was back in the fight, Titch had a clear view of the valve. It was just above his opponent's cockpit. Without even blinking, Titch fired a volley of NailStormers. He watched through the viewfinder as they sailed across the swamp, and was dimly aware of the pilot behind the smoked glass trying desperately to get clear. Titch was horrified to see the first needle explode before it reached its target. It was the second that brought a grin to his face. The needle made a direct hit and exploded with a bang. Even so, AntiGrav stayed above the surface of the water, rotating at a furious pace.

'Congratulations,' said the onboard computer.

'But nothing has happened,' complained Titch.

'Just keep watching.'

At first, just a panel peeled away from AntiGrav's spinning lower limbs. It looked like a knee plate, but Titch found it hard to tell as the part sliced through the air. Then another component shook free, followed by another... and that's when both legs fragmented.

'Whoa!' cried Titch, as the surface of the water from one side of the swamp to the other detonated with flying debris. 'That's a spectacular way to lose!'

With no means of supporting itself in the air, AntiGrav's upper torso plopped uselessly into the water and then capsized upon its back. A second later, the hatch exploded outwards as the pilot operated the ejector seat. Titch watched the figure soar up into the sky before the parachute snapped open.

'You did it!' cried the onboard computer, as the spectators in the grandstand went wild. 'You're top of the leader boards by a long way now!'

'And just a little bit closer to finding out what happened to my father,' Titch said quietly, but his voice was drowned out by the roar from the crowd. 'OK, let's get ourselves to shore and collect the prize money!'

Titch was careful to nurse LoneStar out of the swamp. The mech had been badly damaged by the missile strike and felt very unstable on its feet. Still, it gave him plenty of time to bask in the glory of his victory. Titch beamed proudly as he zoomed in on faces in the stands, including those of Finn and Martha. Then something caught his eye that caused him to frown.

'Hey,' he said, locking the camera on what looked like a furious disagreement between some Championship organisers and a small group of men wearing identical green overalls. 'Isn't that AntiGrav's crew? I recognise them from when they showed up at the guesthouse.' Titch narrowed his eyes and then gasped. 'That's the pilot! I'm sure of it!'

'Then who just ejected from AntiGrav?' asked the onboard computer.

Titch had already pulled the camera out of the zoom. He swung the mech

around, spotted the figure parachuting out of the sky, and followed his descent. The figure could be seen furiously pulling on the cords in a bid to avoid a clump of trees on the banks of the swamp. Whoever it was didn't look very skilled at landing. Rather than clear the trees, his parachute snagged on the upper branches. It left him dangling uselessly.

'Get me out of here, fellas!' the pilot

cried, while kicking and twisting in a bid to break free.

'It's Wyatt Thorne!' declared Titch. 'He must've thought that by secretly piloting AntiGrav he could beat me and collect the prize money!' He focused on Wyatt once more, only for his attention to be drawn to a buzzing sound coming out of a nearby creek. 'And that must be the Wired Bunch!' he declared, spotting an airboat skimming across the water with a dozen rough-looking men on board. At the back of the vessel was a big, fan-like engine that propelled the boat towards the stranded outlaw.

'He might not get the prize money now, but he's going to get away,' said the onboard computer.

'Not if I have anything to do with it,' muttered Titch, pushing LoneStar towards the trees.

The mech moved slowly, dragging its

damaged foot through the swamp. As the airboat neared the trees, it looked like Wyatt really was going to escape. Some of the organisers and AntiGrav's crew were also making their way towards him, but with so many spectators crowding the banks there was no way they would get to him in time.

'Hurry!' cried Wyatt, as the airboat arrived and began to circle. 'Cut me down from here!'

One of the men in the boat produced a switchblade. But just as he reached up for the cords, something leaped from the water with such force that it tipped the boat over. With its jaws open wide, the alligator snapped at the outlaw's heels before plunging back into the depths.

'I've seen that beast before!' said Titch, who was fighting to keep the staggering mech upright. 'And there's its buddy on the bank.'

Sure enough, the second alligator had just crawled out through the reeds. It was enough to persuade the men in the water to turn and swim away as fast as they could. Still dangling from the snagged parachute, Wyatt Thorne watched his Wired Bunch abandon him with an air of utter disgust. 'Call yourself bandits?' he yelled, and yelped as the alligator made another attempt to grab him. 'Help! Help!'

'You'll reach him in thirty point two seconds exactly,' said the onboard computer. 'It would've been ten seconds if Wyatt hadn't hit us with the AirScythe!'

'Let's hope he hangs around long enough for us to rescue him,' said Titch, over the warning beeps and alarms that filled the cockpit.

Wyatt Thorne didn't look happy at the sight of the damaged mech that sloshed through the swamp towards him. But as the alligator snapped at his boot spurs

once more, even he could see that he had to accept the offer of help. Carefully, Titch outstretched one of LoneStar's massive metal hands and wrapped it around the bandit. The mech then plucked Wyatt from the trapped parachute cords as if he were an apple.

'You can unhand me now!' grumbled the outlaw. 'Put me down immediately!'

'If you say so,' said Titch through the loudspeaker.

The second alligator remained on the bank of the swamp. It watched with interest as the mech stepped forward as if to set the bandit on dry ground.

When Wyatt twisted around and saw what awaited him, he began to whimper and struggle. 'OK, don't put me down. I've changed my mind!'

As he said this, AntiGrav's real crew arrived on the bank, though they kept their distance from the alligator. Together with the organisers who had followed them round the swamp, they helped the Wired Bunch out of the murky water. When the sheriff arrived on the scene, along with a couple of lawmen, none of the bandits attempted to run. They looked like their leader: defeated and humiliated.

'It wasn't supposed to end this way!' moaned Wyatt Thorne when Titch finally dumped him at the feet of the sheriff. 'I wanted to teach you a lesson in the battleground – crush you for daring to steal back Martha without paying the ransom.'

'So it was you who fired at us out in the badlands?' Titch had just climbed out of the cockpit. He leaned against the handrail and looked down at the gathering below. 'You know you've ruined one of your own spider mechs, don't you?'

'I could've bought myself a dozen new machines if I'd beaten you on the battleground and collected the prize money.' Miserably, Wyatt Thorne looked up at the sheriff, who had just placed a firm hand on his shoulder. 'Now I've got nothing to look forward to but jail time.'

Just then, Martha and Finn squeezed through the gathering crowd. Titch spotted them straightaway. He waved cheerily. 'We did it, guys! LoneStar took a beating, but we've come out on top again!'

'It'll only get tougher,' grumbled Wyatt Thorne, as the sheriff and his lawmen began to lead the bandits away. 'You can't keep winning, Titch Darwin!' he added, twisting around with a menacing scowl. 'There'll come a time soon when a Championship mech really will show you up for being nothing more than a weedy kid. If it can't be me then it'll be a proper contender. And boy, I'd love to see your father's face when that happens!'

Titch took a moment for Wyatt's words to sink in. 'Wait!' he called out, as the sheriff led the bandits through the crowd. 'Do you mean my dad is alive?'

Wyatt Thorne glanced around and smirked, and then he was lost from sight.

Without drawing breath to call out again, Titch activated the mech's steps. As both alligators slipped away into the water, scared off by so many people, Titch attempted to push his way through the throng. Many spectators had been drawn by the drama, but lots had come for a close up view of LoneStar. It made catching up with Wyatt impossible.

'Let it go, Titch.' This was Finn, who placed a comforting hand on his arm. 'Wyatt knows how to wind you up, that's all.'

'You can't believe a word he says,' added Martha, who joined them now. 'He's probably just hoping to distract you before the next Championship weekend. We've all seen what can happen when you lose focus on doing your best inside the cockpit. It's important that we learn from that. Forget what he said.'

Titch listened carefully to their advice, but he couldn't help play over Wyatt's words. Sure he'd come on the Battle Championship trail to win, but more than that, he had come to find out what had happened to his dad. He just hadn't considered the possibility that he may well still be alive! Titch continued to stare in the direction that the bandits had been taken. Could it really be true? Finally, he sighed and faced his friends.

'OK,' he said. 'I'll let it go for now,' he agreed. 'But I'm not giving up on the hunt to find out what happened to my father. I may have only just discovered the place where he went missing, but even that feels like a big deal to me. Whether he's dead or alive, I feel that I'm getting closer.'

For a moment, the three friends watched the crowds get up close to their fighting machine. LoneStar's left leg was badly damaged. The hole left by the missile was sparking from the inside.

'That's going to take some fixing before we head back off on the trail,' said Martha with a sigh. 'Not to mention a thorough clean. It'll cost us most of the prize money, for sure.'

'We'll just have to save up for a holiday

another day,' joked Finn.

Titch raised his gaze to the mech's visor. He had powered down LoneStar before climbing out of the cockpit. Even so, he figured the onboard computer was still listening, because the two red lights behind the visor flashed on, winked at him, and then faded out once more.

'Whatever it costs,' said Titch, who felt nothing but pride for his battle-scarred but much-loved machine. 'It's vital that LoneStar is in the very best shape for the next Battle Championship weekend.'

'It takes place in docklands on the outskirts of a city, and I just know it's going to be epic,' said Finn, clapping Titch on the back. 'It always is, with you in the cockpit!'

Titch grinned and shrugged. 'I couldn't have done it alone,' he said. 'Without you guys, I'd be just another kid with big dreams but no way to make them come true.'

Martha exchanged a knowing glance with her twin brother. Then she beamed at Titch.

'Isn't that what friends are for?' she reminded him.

• • •